RUBY CELEBRATES!
The Rosh Hashanah Recipe

Laura Gehl

illustrated by
Olga and Aleksey Ivanov

Albert Whitman & Company
Chicago, Illinois

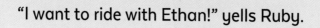

"I want to ride with Ethan!" yells Ruby.

"I want to ride with Ruby!" shouts Avital.

"I want to ride with Avital!" hollers Ethan.

"Me, me, me!" screams Ruby's brother, Benny.

"Okay, you can all ride together with Ethan's moms in their minivan." Dad laughs.

"And Boaz," Ethan adds.

"Right," Dad says. "You can have a nice LOUD ride to the apple orchard, and I'll have a nice QUIET ride with Uncle Jake."

"Last one to the orchard is a rotten apple!" Uncle Jake yells, leaping out of Dad's car and sprinting ahead.

The four cousins and Boaz run after him, giggling and barking. When the others finally catch up...

"What's so funny?" Dad asks.

"You're the rotten apples," Ruby says. "You're like THIS!"

"Oh yeah?" Dad replies. "Well, I say the last one to fill their basket is a rotten apple!"

"Grown-ups against kids," Ruby says. "Go!"

Ruby and her cousins pick apples as fast as they can.

"We win!" Ruby yells. "The grown-ups are the rotten apples!"

"With worms in them," Ethan adds.

Aunt Sharon looks at the overflowing baskets. "We have a LOT of apples."

"We were going to make apple cake for Rosh Hashanah," Dad says. "But I think we might have a few extra..."

Back at Ruby's house, the cousins wash all the apples.

"Yuck! Wash this one again," Avital says, handing Ruby an apple. "Boaz licked it."

"So what should we make with all these apples?" Dad asks. "Apple pie? Apple crisp? Applesauce?"

"Let's make up our own recipes!" Ruby says. "We can have a cooking show!"

"Yes!" the cousins agree.

"And my parents can be our helpers," Avital offers, waving to her mom and dad walking up the driveway.

With Avital's parents and Uncle Jake as their sous-chefs, the cousins get to work trying new recipes...

"Daddy, you're splashing batter everywhere!"

...taste testing...

"Bleh—too much salt," Uncle Jake says.

...and choosing a name for their show.

Later that evening, the whole family gathers.

"Hello," Ethan says. "I'm Chef Appleman, and I will show you how to make apple lasagna!"

"Hello," Avital says. "I'm Chef Applestein, and I will teach you how to make apple pancakes."

"Hello," Ruby says. "I am Chef Appleberg, and I will demonstrate how to make apple pizza!"

"Apple, apple, apple!" yells Benny.

The show was a big hit, with suspense...

"Benny, don't drop the pizza dough!"

...free samples for the audience...

"Do we need to try it?" Zayde whispers.

...and plenty of drama.

"Oh no, Boaz ate two of the pancakes!"

"This is actually delicious!" Zayde admits.

"We should have all these dishes for Rosh Hashanah," Bubbe agrees.

On Rosh Hashanah, the family meets at their synagogue for the morning service.

They pray, sing, and listen to the shofar.

Back at Bubbe and Zayde's house, it's time to eat.

There is round challah with raisins.

Honey for a sweet New Year.

And plenty of apples!

"I'm so full," Dad groans.

Aunt Sharon agrees. "Me too. But at least we polished off all those apples."

"Actually," Avital says, "there are some apples left."

"Let's give them to the Silvermans," Ruby suggests.

Avital and Ethan pack up apples and honey while Ruby makes a card.

The cousins walk the basket next door.

"We hope you have a very sweet New Year!" Ruby says.

"Thank you," Mrs. Silverman replies.
"And Shana Tova!"

"NOW we used all the apples." Ruby plops into Bubbe's armchair.

But Uncle Jake holds out a small bowl. "We forgot about these—the apple centerpiece we had on the table!"

"I can help you make applesauce tomorrow," Bubbe offers.

"No!" Ethan moans.

"No, no, no!" Benny echoes.

"I feel like a rotten apple!" Avital wails, clutching her stomach.

"I guess everyone is sick of apples," Uncle Jake says.

"Actually," Ruby replies, "I think there's one member of the family who is still excited about apples..."

"Here, Boaz! Happy New Year!"

A Note about Rosh Hashanah

Rosh Hashanah is the Jewish New Year, which occurs in the fall. Because Rosh Hashanah means "head of the year" in Hebrew, one tradition is to eat a sheep's head or fish head, although this is not common in the United States.

Rosh Hashanah is the first of the Jewish High Holy Days, and many Jews go to synagogue to pray as part of the holiday. The days in between Rosh Hashanah and Yom Kippur (the Jewish Day of Atonement) are used for personal reflection, apologizing to people we have hurt over the past year, and thinking about how to be our best selves moving forward. At Rosh Hashanah services, the shofar, a musical instrument made out of a ram's horn, is blown.

Apple picking can be a fun holiday activity, because Jewish families dip apples in honey on Rosh Hashanah and say a special prayer. The honey signifies a sweet New Year ahead. Apple cake and honey cake are also traditional Rosh Hashanah foods.

While Jewish families eat braided bread called challah on Shabbat (Friday night) every week, they eat round challah on Rosh Hashanah to signify the cycle of seasons going around each year. The round challah is often filled with raisins, and may be sweeter than usual, again to signify a sweet New Year.

Mrs. Silverman says "Shana Tova" to Ruby and her cousins. This is a Rosh Hashanah greeting meaning "A good year." A longer greeting is "Shana Tova Umetukah," which means "A good and sweet year."

Ruby's Savory Apple Pizza Recipe

Ingredients

14 oz pizza dough, store-bought or homemade

2 apples, cored and sliced thin

8 oz cheddar cheese, shredded

2 tbs walnuts, chopped

2 tbs olive oil

Directions

1. Preheat oven to 475°F. If using a pizza stone, place in oven to heat for about 20 minutes prior to placing pizza on it.

2. Roll out the pizza dough.

3. Brush the dough with olive oil.

4. Spread the cheddar cheese over the pizza dough.

5. Arrange the sliced apples on top of the cheese.

6. Sprinkle the chopped walnuts on top.

7. Have an adult remove the preheated pizza stone from the oven, place the pizza on it, and put back in the oven.

8. Bake the pizza approximately 15 minutes or until edges are golden brown.

Ruby's Sweet Apple Pizza Recipe

Ingredients for sugar cookie crust

1 stick unsalted butter, room temperature

¾ cups sugar

1 ½ cups all-purpose flour

1 egg

1 tsp baking powder

1 tsp vanilla

¼ tsp salt

Ingredients for topping

8 oz cream cheese, softened to room temperature

¼ cups honey

½ tsp vanilla

4–5 cups sliced apples

2 tbs brown sugar

½ tsp cinnamon

Directions

1. Preheat the oven to 350°F.

2. Beat the sugar and butter in a large bowl for 1 to 2 minutes. Add the vanilla and egg. Beat until mixed well. Add the flour, baking powder, and salt. Mix until just combined.

3. Press dough onto a greased 12-inch pizza pan or a cookie sheet. Bake for approximately 20 minutes, or until edges are slightly brown.

4. Let the crust cool completely before topping.

5. In a mixing bowl, beat cream cheese, honey, and vanilla together until fluffy. Spread mixture over sugar cookie crust.

6. Arrange sliced apples on top of cream cheese spread.

7. In a small bowl, combine brown sugar and cinnamon. Sprinkle mixture over top of the pizza.

To Linda, with love and thanks for many sweet memories—LG

To all children, who like to celebrate!—OI & AI

Library of Congress Cataloging-in-Publication data
is on file with the publisher.

Text copyright © 2022 by Laura Gehl
Illustrations copyright © 2022 by Albert Whitman & Company
Illustrations by Olga and Aleksey Ivanov
First published in the United States of America in 2022 by Albert Whitman & Company
ISBN 978-0-8075-7171-2 (hardcover)
ISBN 978-0-8075-7172-9 (ebook)

Printed in China
10 9 8 7 6 5 4 3 2 1 WKT 26 25 24 23 22

For more information about Albert Whitman & Company,
visit our website at www.albertwhitman.com.